I Want to Be a Pilot

Written by Peter J

Peter J. always dreamed of writing stories to inspire children to follow their dreams. Although his career originally took him down other paths, Peter eventually succeeded in becoming a children's book author. He hopes his books will encourage young readers to always believe in themselves. When he's not writing, Peter enjoys reading, traveling, and spending time outdoors. He lives in Chicago with his wife and two kids. Peter looks forward to continuing to write uplifting books that share positive messages with children.

Meet Alex. Ever since Alex can remember, there has been nothing more exciting than watching the big airplanes take off into the clouds. "That's going to be me someday," he dreamed. "I'm going to be a pilot who gets to fly those huge planes!"

Alex loves to imagine and dream about adventure, floating in the sky in a balloon. These dreams fill him with even more excitement to become a pilot.

Alex began reading everything he could to learn about airplanes. How did those enormous jets fly through the air? What made them able to lift off the ground?

On Alex's 9th birthday, his aunt, who was an amateur pilot, surprised him by taking him on his first ride in a small four-seater airplane. Alex could barely contain his excitement as he buckled himself into the co-pilot seat while Aunt Susan went through all the pre-flight checks. Up in the clouds, Aunt Susan let Alex help steer using the flight controls. The birthday boy felt one step closer to his dream of becoming a real pilot someday.

Alex couldn't believe it. Here he was, sitting at the controls in the cockpit of a real plane. The houses and cars below looked tiny as he rose through puffy white clouds. After the flight, Alex told Aunt Susan: "When I grow up, I want to be a pilot just like you!"

After Alex's amazing first flight with Aunt Susan, he loved planes even more. He read lots of books about famous pilots and watched videos of big planes taking off with many people inside. The loud engines and strong power of those giants amazed Alex. Right now, he worked hard in school and played flight games, made model planes, and looked up whenever jets flew by, fascinated.

Alex learned a lot about airplanes and did well in school. He really liked science and math. When he turned 18, it was time for flight school! Alex was so excited as he packed his bags and went to the aviation academy. He was ready to learn how to be a pilot. Looking at all the planes and runways, Alex knew this was where dreams came true. In the first class, they talked about flying, and Alex listened carefully, writing down everything about how planes work and what the weather does.

Over the next year at flight school, when not reading books, Alex spent every spare minute out on the airfield. He learned how to do walk-around inspections of planes, checking tire pressure, fluid levels, and looking for any damage.

One clear evening, Alex flew high above the coastline to watch the sun set over the ocean waters. Then it hit him. "This is the life," he thought to himself. Hands confidently on the controls, Alex turned the wings perfectly to fly in broad curves across the darkening sky. "This is what dreams are made of," Alex thought with a happy sigh. Up there, fully in command of the aircraft, Alex knew the long journey to become a pilot was truly worth it.

After two years of lots of learning, studying late into the night, practicing on a flight simulator, and flying for real, it was finally here - test day! Alex took a big breath, made a wish, and sat in the pilot's seat for the important test. When he landed, the person testing him smiled and said, 'Congratulations, you passed with flying colors - you're officially a licensed pilot!' It was a bit hard to believe after dreaming about it for so long. Alex quickly called his mom and aunt, who were really, really proud.

Pilot Alex took to the skies whenever he could over the next few years, flying regional routes and building up flight hours towards a commercial pilot career. As he gained more aviation experience, the captain let Alex make the full flight announcement.

Years later, Alex proudly walked into the airport ready for a big career milestone - commanding a passenger jet as captain for the very first time!

Alex flew planes for a really long time until he stopped. One quiet night, as he sat in the plane, he felt happy and sad. Alex was proud because the airplane industry kept getting better during his long career. Flying felt like being at home, each flight carving out new paths forward. The end.

This book was inspired by Peter J's uncle. It shows that anyone can achieve their dreams by doing what they love and giving their best effort.

The Wright brothers, Orville and Wilbur Wright, are credited with inventing and building the world's first successful powered airplane. They achieved the first controlled, sustained flight with a powered, heavier-than-air aircraft on December 17, 1903, near Kitty Hawk, North Carolina, USA.

Peter J wholeheartedly cheers on every child with dreams, urging them to follow their passions, and sincerely hopes that their dreams come true. If you enjoy Peter J's book, we would truly appreciate your feedback in the form of a review and a star rating. Your thoughts and ratings mean a lot, as Peter J is committed to creating even more enjoyable books for your reading delight. Thank you wholeheartedly for your ongoing support.

Made in the USA
Middletown, DE
23 October 2024

63170241R00022